Love, Nash, Finn & Beau,
Be Courageous!
—Marin

Scary

the
Scared Iguana

Featuring the Creatures
of the Florida Keys

by Marin Resnick

Illustrated by Eric Labacz

First published in paperback by Marin Resnick in August of 2019.

©2019 by Marin Resnick.

Scary the Scared Iguana & Scary the Iguana & Scary (as it pertains to the iguana noted in this book or merchandise) are trademarks of Marin Resnick.

Books may be purchased for business of promotion use for special sales. For more information contact ScaryTheIguana@gmail.com or visit https://www.ScaryTheIguana.com.

Printed in Logan, Iowa.

Book Design & Illustration by Eric Labacz, www.LabaczDesign.com.

ISBN 978-0-578-42773-7 paperback

Distributed to the trade by Onyx Dog Enterprise LLC.

National Iguana Day is the second Saturday in September.

For Walter, who always encourages me.

Scary the Iguana was a scary looking fellow. His teeth were long and his eyes were yellow.

But, despite his long jaws and black claws, Scary was afraid of everything.

Scary lived by a rock, under a dock, next
to the waters of the Blue Hole in
Big Pine Key in the Florida Keys.

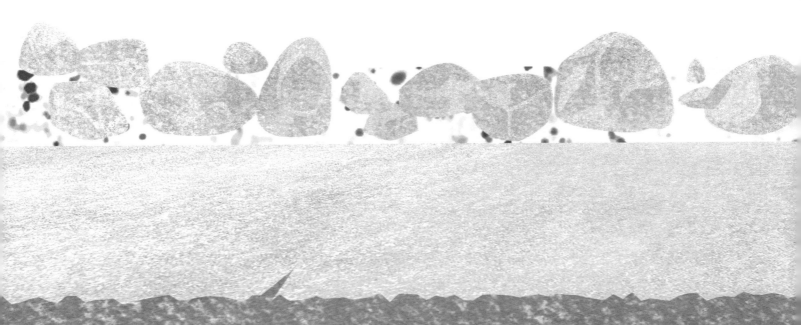

Many of the **Key's critters** could be found
living in the Blue Hole.

Scary's friends, Penny the Pelican,
Annie the Alligator and Tommy the
Turtle all lived in the Blue Hole too.

One day, Scary came out from under his rock,

sat on the dock, and warmed himself

in the sun.

SCARY!

"Scary!," Penny called
from her perch.

aaaaaaaaaahhhhhhh!

Scary screamed, and ran back under his rock.

Penny flew down from her perch and stood next to Scary.

"Scary, why do you scare so easily?,"
she asked. "I don't know," Scary said
as he hung his head in shame.
Penny flew back up to her perch.

Later on, Scary came out from behind
his rock and went back up on the dock to
warm himself in the sun again.

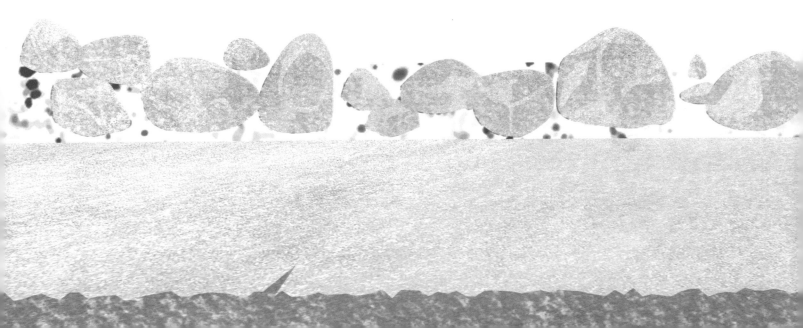

Helloooo!

Annie peered out from behind a bush,
next to the dock. "Hello Scary!,"
she screamed.

Scary was so scared he **scuttled**

right back behind his rock.

Annie looked up at
Penny, who was still
on her perch.

"Our friend is so scared of everything,"
Annie said sadly.

"I know," Penny said.

She was upset too.

A little while later, Scary came back out from behind his rock and went to the edge of the dock to look for Tommy.

But when a fish jumped out of the water and frightened Scary, he ran away again.

Penny, Annie and Tommy saw
Scary scurry away.

"Why is Scary so scared of
everything?," Tommy asked.
"I wish we could help our
friend find his courage."

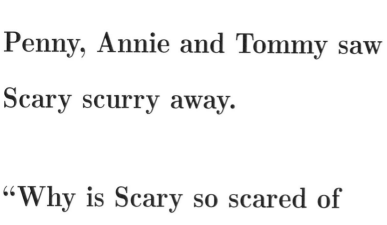

All of a sudden, the sky turned grey and
the **wind** began to **whirl.**

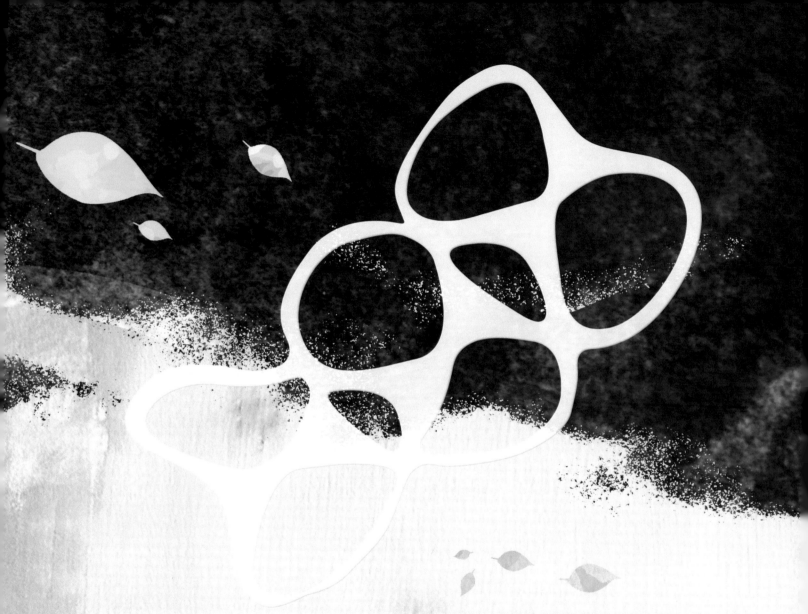

Tommy lifted his head up to see what was
happening when a **plastic ring** blowing in
the wind got caught around his **head.**

"Help!," Tommy yelled.
"I'm stuck and **I** can't get out!"

HELP!

To save Tommy, Scary didn't have time to be scared.

He ran quickly, jumped into the water, and grabbed

Tommy by his tail.

Scary pulled Tommy up onto the shore. He grabbed the plastic ring with his sharp teeth and claws and used them to free Tommy!

"You saved Tommy!," Penny exclaimed, as all of the Key critters cried with joy.

HOORAY!

Scary held his head high, as he and his friends stayed on the dock and pitched rocks into the waters of the Blue Hole.

His friends were happy and smiled. They knew that Scary had finally found his courage.

The Florida Keys

The Florida Keys are a group of tropical islands located just south of Miami, Florida, and about 90 miles north of Cuba.

Big Pine Key is the most unique key of the keys as it is the home of the National Key Deer Refuge where the Key Deer live. It is also the home the Blue Hole. The Blue Hole is an abandoned quarry which filled with fresh water from a hurricane. This, now fresh water lake, attracted two American Alligators who now call it home along with many other fresh water creatures including turtles and fish. Many visitors of the Keys go to the hole to watch the alligators, safely, from a dock. There are also deer scattered around the hole, who come there looking for plants to eat and water to drink.

Florida

Miami

Key Largo

Key West

Big Pine Key

– Creatures of the Florida Keys –

Iguanas: Iguanas came to the Keys as stowaways on ships coming from South America. This makes iguanas an invasive species in the Keys.

Pelicans: Both brown and white pelicans live in the Florida Keys. But, brown pelicans live in the Keys year round while the white pelicans migrate to the Midwest during the summer. Many brown pelicans can be found by fisherman and docks looking for fish to eat. There are many at Robbie's Marina, where visitors can go feed large fish called tarpon.

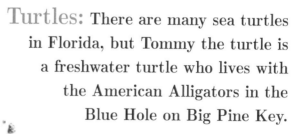

Turtles: There are many sea turtles in Florida, but Tommy the turtle is a freshwater turtle who lives with the American Alligators in the Blue Hole on Big Pine Key.

Alligators: Alligators are freshwater reptiles. The only place alligators are found in the Florida Keys is the Blue Hole on Big Pine Key. But, there are many crocodiles living in the salt waters of the Keys, which can be seen sunning themselves on docks or on the beach.

About the Author

Marin Resnick is a writer and photographer who enjoys the urban-country lifestyle of Hunterdon County, New Jersey. Marin and her daughter, JR, enjoy spending summers on the shores of Islamorada, Florida watching the real Scary the iguana sun himself on their dock and run away when they try to feed him bananas. They also enjoy their trips to the Blue Hole in Big Pine Key, Florida where they walk the trails and look for alligators and turtles.

This is Marin's debut book.

When not chasing the reptiles of the Florida Keys, JR spends lots of time with her favorite furry friend, Mino, the pony.

About the Illustrator

Eric Labacz runs a small design studio from his home in Bucks County, Pa., where he lives with his wife and their four year old son. He loves animals and all sorts of reptiles. Eric designs book covers for publishers and self-publishing authors and has worked in all types of genres. Though he has illustrated for books before, this is his first time illustrating an entire children's book. He had a lot of fun getting to know Scary and his friends. For more information, visit his site at: www.LabaczDesign.com.